A GOLDEN BOOK • NEW YORK

This special edition was printed for Kohl's Department Stores, Inc.
(for distribution on behalf of Kohl's Cares, LLC, its wholly owned subsidiary)
by Random House Children's Books, a division of Penguin Random House LLC, New York.

KOHL'S
Style 18033
Factory Number 126509
Production Date 01/2020

Ages 3 and up

MANUFACTURED IN CHINA
10 9 8 7 6 5 4 3 2 1

I'm a UNICORN

By Mallory C. Loehr
Illustrated by Joey Chou

I am moonlight white.
I have a magical horn.
I look a lot like a horse, of course.

I'm a UNICORN!

My horn can make water clean . . .

. . . or heal a hurt.

I can be strong and fierce.

I can be sweet and gentle.

I frolic in the forest.

I prance
in the fields.

I am a force of nature—

I'm a UNICORN!

Sometimes I gallop
with my herd.

We play hide-and-seek.

Can you find us all?

Other times,
I love to be alone

in the quiet of dawn.
Shhh. . . .

I am magic.
I am mystery.

I'm a
UNICORN!

Do you believe in me?

I believe in you!

I'm a
Ballerina!

By Sue Fliess

Illustrated by Joey Chou

*B*allet lessons! Time to go—
We head for the studio!

First we balance on the barre,
Leaning over, reaching far,

Stretching arms and legs out long.
Ballet dancers must be strong!

Five positions in ballet—

second position

first position

We'll review them
all today!

third position

fourth
position

fifth position

Next we plié and chassé,
Pirouette, petit jeté.

We've been working hard all year.
Our recital's finally here!

Last rehearsal for the show—
Get it right from

head

to

toe.

Twist my hair up in a bun—
Getting dressed is half the fun!
Tutu, tights, a crown, some bows . . .

Mom puts powder on my nose.
Ballet slippers for my feet.
Now my costume is complete!

My recital starts at eight.
"Hurry up! We can't be late!"

The music is about to start!
"What if I forget my part?"
"Take some deep breaths.
    You'll be great!"
I breathe in and
    stand up straight.

Fix my tutu. Tug my tights.
My instructor dims the lights.

We hope our show will be a hit!
Curtains open . . . this is it!

That's my number.
Here I go. . . .
I can't believe
I'm in a show!

Gracefully we bend and rise,
Arms like wings of butterflies.

Perfectly I pirouette!
But the show's not over yet. . . .

Glide and twirl, leap . . . and land.
All the parents clap and stand!

Time for me to take a bow.
I'm a ballerina now!

I'm a Narwhal

By Mallory C. Loehr
Illustrated by Joey Chou

I am **NOT** a unicorn.

I am NOT a fish.

I'm a **narwhal!**

I look magical,
but I'm really just
a kind of whale.

My closest relatives
are the beluga whale,
the dolphin,
and the porpoise.

I live in the cold Arctic waters
with my pod, or family.

I can dive very deep
and hold my breath
under the ice for a long time!

In the spring, narwhals
swim to warmer bays.
This is called migration.

Once there, we like to lie on the water's surface and rest. This is called logging!

Long ago, when narwhal horns
were found on the beach,

people thought they were
magical unicorn horns.

Wouldn't you?

My horn is actually
a big front tooth, or tusk.
It grows in a spiral—
right through my upper lip!

It helps me "taste" the salt
in the water
and find the right places to hunt.

Boy narwhals are usually
the ones with tusks,
but some girls have them, too!

Because I'm a narwhal,
I can stun a tasty codfish
or squid with my tusk—
then suck the meal into my mouth!

I communicate with clicking and knocking sounds.

Humans don't know
what I'm saying,
but my friends and family do!

I may not be a unicorn, but I am magical in my own way...